The Moon Drinkers

THE MOON SHIVER SERIES
BOOK TWO

The Moon Drinkers

Melanie Winter

SIBLING
PRESS

Sibling Press
Level 2, Titchfield House
69/85 Tabernacle Street
London
EC2A 4RR

www.sibling-press.com

First Edition 2009

British Library in Cataloguing in Publication Data
A catalogue record for this book is available from the British Library

ISBN: 978-1-906847-01-2

Cover illustration by Peter Ferguson
Text illustrations by Steve Crisp
Book and cover design by Ian Hughes
Edited by Katherine Fry

Printed in the United Kingdom by CPI Mackays, Chatham ME5 8TD

Chapter 1

Stealing Moonlight

The night was clear and the full moon shone pale and silver over the deserted beach. Waves rolled steadily onto the sand, each breaker pulling the ocean further up the beach with the incoming tide.

Wissen waited in the darkness, hidden by the rocks and shadows at the base of the cliff. His long dark coat swept over his high black boots and his thick silver hair glinted faintly in the moonlight. He was sure that the Moon Drinkers would come soon.

For many months Wissen had secretly watched them. He had seen them leap, nimble as mountain goats, from rock to rock on the steep slopes and cliffs edging the beach. He had watched them in the moonlight when they glowed like lanterns, and he had watched them during the day when they were almost invisible, their colours changing and blending with their

surroundings. Wissen had seen the Moon Drinkers come onto the Muddlemarsh beach when the tide was high and the moon was full. He knew that somehow they drew their power from the moonlight and he was determined to find out how. He wanted the power of the Moon Drinkers.

Wissen bit his thumbnail as he waited. He had hidden as close as he dared to the hollow in the sand dunes where the Moon Drinkers gathered. The moon rose higher, but still there was no sign of them. He stared intently over the ocean rolling under the moonlight.

'Where are they?' he muttered impatiently.

The moon was high in the eastern sky before he saw them, riding upright in the crests of the waves, finding a foothold in the water. They shone faintly with the light of the moon, as white as the spray scattering around them. The Moon Drinkers rode the rolling breakers right onto the beach and glided easily onto the sand, the foam swirling and bubbling around their feet.

They gathered at the edge of the water and then turned and walked up the beach to the hollow in the dunes.

Wissen scrambled to the top of a large rock near the hollow and peered down at the Moon Drinkers. They were sitting in a circle deep in the hollow. Only the tallest Moon Drinker remained standing. Except for a faint moonlit radiance they blended almost perfectly into the night-faded colour of the sand.

The tall Moon Drinker turned and knelt in front of a large flat-topped rock at the back of the sandy hollow. Bending forward, she dug in the sand under the rock and pulled out a soft leather bag. She tipped it on to a cloth on the sand. A small pile of pearls shimmered in the moonlight. She reached again under the rock and pulled out a second bag. Soon a pile of rose quartz lay next to the pearls. Two more Moon Drinkers joined her and, kneeling in the centre of the circle, they began to drop the pearls and quartz into something that looked very much like a coffee grinder. Slowly they turned the handle. A shimmering pink powder trickled into a silver dish.

When the grinding was done, the tall Moon Drinker moved gracefully around the circle, trickling a small handful of the powder into the silver flagons that each Moon Drinker held out.

Following behind her, a second Moon Drinker added a clear liquid poured from a large silver ewer. When this was done, they raised their flagons to the moon and drank.

Wissen watched as a circle of moonbeams brightened around the Moon Drinkers until they were encased in a cone of moonlight. Then the circle was gone, but the glow of the Moon Drinkers remained, strong and bright. The Moon Drinkers skipped nimbly out of the hollow, dancing over the sand and down to the water's edge.

Wissen spoke softly to himself. 'Pearls and quartz. That's how they steal the power of the moon.' He wondered what liquid was in their flagons that completed the mixture.

The Moon Drinkers were kicking and splashing in the foamy shallows. Wissen climbed down from the rock and tiptoed towards the hollow. He cursed the sand as his boots squeaked with each step.

At the edge of the hollow, Wissen crouched down and pressed against the sandy slope of the dune. He looked around. The Moon Drinkers were all down at the water's edge. Sure that no one was watching him, he slid down to the bottom of the hollow.

Wissen dug under the rock with both hands until he felt the leather bag. He pulled it out and opened it; a handful of pearls nestled inside. His excitement growing, Wissen again scrabbled around in the sand under the rock, feeling for the bag of rose quartz. His hand closed on the leather pouch and tugged it free. Gleefully, he opened the pouch and looked inside. It was empty.

Wissen cursed. Now that he knew the secret, he wanted the power of the moon. He had to have it. It was his right to have it, he told himself. He grabbed the bag of pearls, remembering just in time to take the grinder, and ran into the darkness of the overhanging cliffs. Hidden from the moonlight, he sat and brooded.

'I wonder what else I could use instead of rose quartz?' He considered the possibilities. 'Sand? Shells? Rocks?' Then he laughed quietly. 'Of course. Why didn't I think of it earlier?' He reached into his pocket and pulled out a large leather pouch.

'Black powder!' he exclaimed, feeling the weight of the heavy pouch in his hand. 'Surely much better than stupid rose quartz.'

Wissen thought back to how he had found the shiny black powder in the caves of the High Mountains and then experimented with it in his laboratory. By itself the black powder had been disappointing, but when mixed with other materials the results had been spectacular. Ground with certain plants, the black powder gave off odorous vapours that breathed fear and loneliness or a dangerous euphoria into those that inhaled them. When mixed with other minerals the black powder formed crystals which grew into fantastic shapes in a dozen different jewel colours. Wissen had even managed to concoct a very exciting explosive. Of course, some of the experiments, particularly the one that had produced a pretty, sweet-tasting liquid of a clear and vivid pink, had been much less satisfying.

Sheltered by the cliffs, hidden from the Moon Drinkers on the beach, Wissen poured some of the pearls into the mouth of the grinder, adding a generous sprinkling of black powder. He was just about to start grinding when he thought of something. He pulled a handkerchief out of his pocket and spread it under the grinder. Then he gripped its handle firmly and turned it. Every now and then a tiny spark flew out. Wissen smiled as he collected the glittering speckled dust.

After ten minutes of hard work a miniature dune of gritty powder lay on the handkerchief. That should be enough, Wissen thought, and tipped the powder into his water flask. He shook the flask vigorously. He unscrewed the cap of the flask and took a long, deep drink. The gritty mix tasted metallic and bitter.

Twitching with excitement, Wissen waited to feel the power of the moon pour into his body. He waited to feel taller and stronger. He waited to see the glow of moonlight shine out from his body. He waited – not unhopefully – to become more handsome. He waited a long time, but nothing happened. Realising that the experiment had failed, Wissen stamped his feet, snorting with disappointment and frustration. In the darkness he was unaware of the amethyst vapour curling out of his nose and forming a purple haze around him.

Wissen stuffed the bag of pearls and the pouch of black powder into his pocket and headed back up the cliff to the clearing where he had left his flying machine. The machine was his favourite possession. It was a beautiful, burnished-copper oval; open-topped, flat-rimmed, with two rows of sleek vapour vents underneath. It was as fast as the wind. The glorious perfection of the machine was spoiled by small dents and scratches on its underside. Every time he looked at it Wissen was reminded that one of those annoying and ridiculous Muddles had stolen it and crashed it in a treetop. Wissen had repaired it as best he could, but it still tended to fly a bit to the left. If he didn't pay careful attention, it would go round in circles instead of flying straight.

At the top of the cliffs Wissen stopped to catch his breath. He stood for a moment looking at his flying machine. Scowling, Wissen promised himself that one day he would make those Muddles sorry they had even touched it. He climbed in, started the engine and headed for home.

After a short flight across Muddlemarsh, Wissen landed the machine outside his hut in the forest. He stepped out and sighed noisily. It had been a disappointing night. In the moonlight, he noticed the purple breath misting from his mouth. Looking down his nose, he exhaled an experimental puff of breath. A violet plume billowed out. He made his mouth into an "O" and blew purple smoke rings.

'This looks interesting,' he said to himself. Wissen's grey cat jumped onto the back of the flying machine and began cleaning its paws. Wissen bent over and breathed on it. The cat hissed, then slowly toppled over and lay still. Wissen prodded it, but there was no sign of life. Slowly it slid down the slippery metal into the space behind the driver's seat. 'Stupid cat,' Wissen muttered. He wondered why he had ever bothered to bring the stray cat to Muddlemarsh. At least it wasn't – well, hadn't been – a really irritating Muddle cat.

Wissen wondered if the purple breath would work on people. Looking at his reflection in the polished surface of the flying machine, he exhaled through his nose. Curls of purple smoke flowed dragon-like from his nostrils. He blew out of his mouth and inhaled back in through his nose in a rolling circle of purple smoke. Gradually the colour began to fade until there was not a trace of it when he exhaled.

Wissen considered the possibilities of the purple breath. He really must try the mixture again. He felt the pockets of his jacket; the bag containing the remaining pearls was still there. Maybe the night hadn't been a total waste of time after all.

Wissen went to bed thinking of all the things he might be able to do with his purple breath. But in the morning it was a very different story. He woke feeling sick. His head ached appallingly. The sweet sounds of birds singing outside his window pierced his brain. Wissen yelled at them to shut up, and then wished he hadn't; yelling hurt. Never again, he told himself. Never again was he going to drink that pearl and black powder concoction.

Chapter 2

Wave Rider

It was about three weeks later that Wave strapped his surfboard to his back and pedalled his bike from Home to the beach. Dropping the bike on the sand, Wave tucked the board under his arm and ran into the water. He paddled out to find the perfect wave, which took a while, and then he stood up on his board and fell off, which didn't take long at all.

On his thirteenth wave of the morning, Wave finally managed to stay upright on his board for several seconds and was feeling pleased. He looked around, just in case there was someone watching to appreciate this. He saw something which made his mouth open wide and his eyes open even wider. Riding a wave, effortlessly, gracefully, like part of the wave itself, was a young girl. Where her body met the wave she was as deep green as the ocean, but where she rose up into the breaking foam she was as bright as the spray. For a moment Wave thought it was the wave itself that had shaped itself into a girl. But what made him fall off his board as she surfed next to him were her feet. She was not standing on a surfboard. In fact, she seemed to be standing on some solid part of the wave itself under its breaking crest. Startled, Wave fell off his board and disappeared under the water. When he came up again the girl was gone.

'Man, that was one trippy chick,' Wave said out loud. 'How'd she do that?'

Wave paddled out to catch the next rolling breaker, but his heart wasn't in it; he couldn't stop thinking about the strange girl. Just as he was getting ready for the next wave, a cloud, shaped like a bird and moving quicker than the wind, passed over the sun. Wave's body shimmered and he closed his eyes. The Mix was passing over the Muddles.

Wave opened his eyes and looked down, curious to see what he had got this time, and saw Crimson's bright red fire jacket. He stuck a leg up out of the water. It was covered in ballet tights and a dainty ballet slipper. Wave pointed his toe elegantly, just like a ballerina. Just like Reach, actually.

'Here goes,' thought Wave, as a promising wave approached. He stood up on his board. It felt pretty good.

'Cool,' he said, trying an experimental bend of the knee. 'Kinda works, really.'

Wave came into the beach and lay on the sand. He'd had enough surfing for one day. He stood up and slung his board over his back. Getting on his bike, he pedalled back to Home, Reach's tutu bouncing up and down and Crimson's jacket drying in the wind.

Chapter 3

Strange Days

Muddlemarsh is a beautiful place, and the Muddles have lived there happily for hundreds of years. The neighbouring countries of Myrmidia and Beadledom are beautiful too, and the Muddles and the Beadles and the Myrmidots, despite their differences, share the Land peacefully. That is not to say that the three peoples of the Land always see eye to eye, but they accept one another's peculiarities, each thinking that clearly it is the others who are peculiar. Some mystified head-shaking and comments such as 'I'll never understand them Muddles (or Beadles, or Myrmidots), not if I live to be a hundred and thirty-five!' are the closest they come to disharmony. When faced with trouble, the different peoples of the Land never fail to come to the rescue of their neighbours.

Home is the chief town of Muddlemarsh, and homey is how it feels. The cottages are warm and cosy and the gardens are pretty and fragrant. At any given time of the day it is likely that the smell of freshly brewed coffee and biscuits still warm from the oven will be wafting through the town. The Muddles work only as hard as they need to. After all, as the Muddles themselves would say, there's too much good coffee to drink and too many friends to talk to and too many mouth-watering biscuits to eat to waste unnecessary time working. What more does anyone need? And so generally the Muddles are a happy people and Home is a peaceful place.

But something had changed in Muddlemarsh, and the Muddles were feeling uneasy. Nearly four weeks had passed since the full moon when the Moon Drinkers had danced on the sand and Wissen had stolen their pearls. That full moon had waned and disappeared, and a new moon had risen and was waxing close to the full.

None of the Muddles quite knew why, but a feeling of disquiet shivered through Home. Autumn leaves tumbled and scattered, unable to settle, in a chilly restless wind. Muddles were unusually hurried as they walked through Home, looking over their shoulders and agreeing that something wasn't quite right. Whispers and rumours weaved about the town like cats around ankles.

The wind blew bitingly cold around the steps of the library where Kite and Poke were sitting side by side. Below them Chip was sitting on the bottom step, leaning against the railing. Poke pulled her trench coat tighter round her waist and pushed her wind-tangled red hair back from her face.

Poke frowned as she stared over the main street of Home.

'Everything feels peculiar,' she said, turning to Kite. 'I don't know what, but something is definitely not right.'

'You're just being silly,' replied Kite impatiently, 'always imagining a mystery even when there isn't one.'

'I am not!' said Poke indignantly. 'What about Wave seeing that girl surfing with no board? And Slight finding sand in his magician's hat? And,' she finished triumphantly, 'what about the bitter coffee?'

Kite had no answer to this last one. Two nights ago at Whist's coffee house the coffee had been bitter and tasteless and strangely gritty. All the

Muddles had looked into their cups in disbelief. Then they had looked at each other. No one had dared to look at Whist. The coffee really had been undrinkable. Such a thing had never happened before. Whist never had a bad coffee day.

Kite got to his feet and zipped up his leather flying jacket. 'Well, it doesn't mean there's some mystery in Muddlemarsh. Things just happen. There's no point worrying about it.'

'I can't help worrying about it,' said Poke crossly. 'When things aren't right I want to find out why and I want to fix it.' She looked down at Chip. 'What do you think, Chip? Do you think there's something weird going on in Home?'

Chip, chewing thoughtfully on a piece of grass, looked up at the clouds. 'Hard to say,' he answered finally.

Poke frowned. 'Well, something is definitely odd.'

'Don't tell me,' said Kite, looking down at her, 'you have a gut feeling about this one.'

'Well, I do!' replied Poke. 'So, are you going to help me find out what's going on?'

'Nope.' Kite shook his head. 'I'm not going to waste my time looking for trouble. Anyway, I think I'll get in some flying before dark.' He walked off down the street, whistling cheerfully to prove that everything was just fine.

'Think I'll be going too,' said Chip, standing up and stretching. He smiled and waved lazily back at Poke as he strolled down the street.

Poke sat by herself for a while, her chin resting on her hands, her elbows resting on her knees. Maybe Kite was right; maybe she was just imagining that something was wrong. Calamity came and sat against Poke's legs, resting her head on Poke's knee. After a minute or two she nudged Poke's arm with her nose and let out a sigh.

Poke looked down at the puppy and patted her head. 'Do you think there's something wrong in Muddlemarsh?' she asked Calamity.

Calamity tilted her head and looked up at Poke and growled. 'I don't know, but lately I've had this itch on my back that I just can't seem to scratch.'

Poke scratched the puppy absent-mindedly,

frowning as she looked out across the main street. It looked the same as it always did: the trees nodded and bowed in the cold wind, admiring each other's outfits of bright autumn leaves. The gardens bloomed with autumn flowers and the blue River Meddle trimmed with white lace ripples splashed in its bed. The cottages were as neat and welcoming as ever. But still Poke had the uneasy feeling that something was wrong.

'Shall we go, Calamity?' Poke stood up and began to walk down the main street of Home, the puppy padding along at her side. As they passed the Common, the pile of autumn leaves behind them suddenly rustled and scattered, kicked by invisible feet. Poke turned and looked round. The trunk of the tree nearest to her was ruffled at its base with leaves, motionless now as Poke stared at them. There was something peculiar about the deeply shaded bark on the tree. Poke leaned forward for a better look; she could have sworn there was a very faint outline on the trunk, like someone's shadow stuck on the bark.

'Weird,' Poke said. 'Oh, maybe Kite was right; maybe I'm imagining mysteries around every tree trunk!' She turned to walk on, but Calamity had crouched down and was growling at the tree.

'You coming, Calamity?' Poke called over her shoulder. Calamity gave one last yelp at the tree and ran to follow Poke. Out of the corner of her eye Poke could have sworn she saw the shadow on the bark move very slightly. She spun round and stared at the tree, but there was no one there.

Chapter 4

Uninvited Visitors

Poke woke with her heart pounding. The room was completely dark. She was sure she had heard a noise that was out of place. She lay very still in her bed, waiting to hear or see something. There was nothing but silence and darkness.

Trying not to make a sound, she sat up and looked towards the closed door. A faint creak came from the room beyond. Then, very slowly, a faint pale light edged under the door and spread in a pool over the floor. Poke watched it creep closer to her bed and she drew in a deep sharp breath. It sounded very loud in the silence of the room. The pool of light retreated and slipped back under the door.

Poke wondered whether it was worse waking up not knowing if something was there, or knowing that there was. She swung her legs over the side of the bed and carefully, trying to keep the bed

from squeaking, put her feet on the floor and tiptoed over to the door. She stood in front of it for a moment, unsure if she was brave enough to open it. Holding her breath, she turned the handle and peered around the edge of the door. At exactly the same time she heard a small click and felt the softest wisp of cold air brush past her.

The little sitting room was empty, but Poke was sure that her front door had just opened and shut. Running to the window, she looked out across the misty moonlit garden. A pale light, swaying like a Chinese lantern, was moving through the garden, flitting from tree to tree and weaving through the flower beds. The front gate opened and the light disappeared down the street.

Poke shivered and pulled the curtains shut. The floor felt strangely gritty under her bare feet. She reached down and touched the floor and felt a light sprinkling of sand covering the bare boards. Poke didn't want to go back to bed. Going to her room she slipped on her woolly slippers and robe. She looked at the clock ticking on her bookshelf, four o'clock. Wrapping the robe tightly around her middle, she went into the kitchen and warmed some milk. Sitting in her big easy chair, with her feet tucked under her, she drank warm milk and ate nut-crumble biscuits, and wondered who had come into her house.

The morning took a long time to arrive, but when Poke opened the curtains at last, the garden outside her window was faintly visible. The rising sun struggled to be seen through the damp mist. She felt only slightly more cheerful in the daylight.

Poke looked at the clock; it was nearly eight. She dressed and ate breakfast, and then walked to the Common in the centre of Home.

The damp fog of the early morning was lifting and the autumn sun was surprisingly warm. The bitter wind of the day before was gone. In the garden of Whist's coffee house Muddles were finishing breakfast, enjoying the warmth of the sun on their backs. Younger Muddles were already in the playground at the edge of the Common, and several were listening at the Songpost in the Quad. The long cords trailing from the top of the Songpost were plugged firmly into their ears.

Everything seemed so safe and normal that Poke could hardly believe she had really seen the strange moonlit shape moving through her garden. But the sand she had swept up before leaving her cottage had been real, she reminded herself.

Poke was glad to see Kite and Chip sitting in the bandstand. She walked towards them, past the Songpost where Grunge was listening and playing air guitar. She waved to him and he waved back, his head moving to music that Poke couldn't hear.

Inside the bandstand Kite was sitting with his knees drawn up, resting back against the railing. Chip was leaning over the railing and watching some of the Muddles playing their favourite game, crickle. The sleeves of Chip's checked lumberjack shirt were rolled up to make the most of the warmth from the sun. The tomahawk in his sturdy tool belt glinted in the light.

'Hey,' said Poke, climbing the steps to the bandstand, 'what are you two up to?'

'Nothing much,' Kite answered. 'What about you?'

'Same,' said Poke sitting up on the railing surrounding the bandstand. She stared silently out over the Common.

'OK, what's up?' asked Kite, when Poke didn't speak.

'I don't know.' Poke turned back to the two boys. 'Something scary happened last night.'

'Really? What?' asked Chip.

Poke told them about the noise and the light coming under her door, and the lantern-light figure moving through her garden.

'You sure you weren't dreaming?' asked Kite sceptically.

'Of course I'm sure. I had to sweep up the sand this morning.'

'What do you think it was?' asked Chip.

'I don't really know,' said Poke slowly. 'But I didn't like it.'

'Maybe you spent so much time yesterday thinking that something was going on in Muddlemarsh that you just imagined it,' said Kite.

Poke shook her head vigorously. 'No, it really happened,' she said. 'I'm sure of it.'

'Well, at least nothing bad happened to you,' said Kite. 'What'll we do today?'

'How about a game of crickle?' Chip suggested.

'OK,' agreed Kite.

'No, I don't feel like it,' said Poke. 'Think I'll go for a walk in the forest.' She jumped off the railing of the bandstand and waved goodbye.

Several hours later Poke was sitting on a log in the forest just outside Home. The leaves on the trees were yellow, orange and red, and a carpet of them covered the ground. The clear autumn sky of the morning had clouded over, and a chilly wind had sprung up from the east. Poke pulled her brown beret over her ears and turned up the collar of her trench coat against the cold. She had the same uneasy feeling that she had felt the day before on the steps of the library, and again during the previous night. It was time to go home.

Poke looked up at the sound of leaves crunching softly close by. Leaf was coming towards her, carrying all her camping equipment in the pack on her back. She looked like she'd been crying.

'Hey, Leaf,' Poke called out to her, 'what's wrong?'

'Everything!' Leaf replied.

'That's a lot,' said Poke sympathetically. 'Come and sit down and tell me about it.'

Leaf sat on the log next to Poke.

'Well?' Poke prompted her. 'Tell me what's wrong.'

Leaf sniffed. 'I came back to my tent, and as soon as I stepped inside I could see that something wasn't right. My sleeping bag had been turned inside out and thrown in the middle of the floor. And my beautiful little camp pantry had been tipped over and cups and plates, and forks and knives and spoons were scattered in with my shoes and hankies and some biscuits and, well, everything! Who could have done such a thing? Why?'

'I don't know,' said Poke slowly. 'Seems like a lot of weird things are happening lately.'

'It was such a shock. I just wasn't prepared to see my tent all messed up,' said Leaf, trying to find her handkerchief.

'Never mind, let's go home together,' said Poke, standing up and holding out her hand to Leaf.

Leaf nodded as Poke pulled her to her feet. 'Let's,' she said, sniffing and smiling at the same time. 'I'm glad you're here.'

They walked towards Home, and Poke told Leaf about her visitor of the night before. Leaf shook her head and shuddered.

It was almost dark when they reached Home, and the mist was gathering. The moon was nearly full, but the clouds barely gave it a chance to shine through. Home was a welcome sight; lamplight shone from the windows of the cottages, and the seven street lamps at each of the seven bridges across the River Meddle were aglow.

They didn't expect to see Sky, her silver-white astronaut suit reflecting the light from the street lamp. She was leaning over the parapet of the first bridge and staring intently down at the darkness of the rushing water below.

Poke and Leaf hurried over to her.

'What are you looking at?' asked Poke, as she and Leaf leaned over the parapet and looked into the water.

Sky held up her hand. 'Listen,' she whispered. 'I think someone is crying.' Sky walked quietly down to the riverbank, trying to see where the sound was coming from. In the moonlight she could just make out the shape of a young girl, pearly, shimmering, faintly moonlit, lying face down on the bank of the River Meddle and crying softly.

'Hello,' said Sky. 'What's wrong?'

Startled, the moonlit girl sat up and looked up at Sky. Sky took a step closer and held out her hand, but before she could speak again, the girl rose to her feet and slipped silently into the river. Her feet sank only just beneath the surface as she moved quickly through the rippling water.

'Please don't go!' Sky called out, sliding further down the riverbank after the girl. For a brief moment the girl was visible, a moonlit figure on the Meddle, until a cloud covered the moon and the girl disappeared. Sky stared into the

darkness, but the girl was gone. She turned to walk back up the riverbank. The moon came out from behind the cloud and something on the grass gleamed in the shaft of moonlight. Sky reached down and picked up the shining object before running back up the bank and onto the bridge where Poke and Leaf were waiting. Sky opened her hand. A small and beautiful pearl lay like a tiny full moon in her palm.

'Where did that come from?' asked Poke, raising her eyebrows in surprise.

'I found it where the girl was lying,' Sky answered. 'Did you see her?'

Poke and Leaf shook their heads.

'All we saw was the moonlight shining on the grass,' said Leaf.

'She was there,' said Sky. 'I saw her.' She added to herself, 'And I could feel her there even without seeing her.'

Sky lifted her fingers to lightly touch the rows of black pearls in her ears, before closing her hand tightly around the pearl she had found on the grass. She wondered about the girl she had just seen; who she was, and where she had come from, and why she felt so drawn to her.

Leaf and Poke looked at each other, and then at Sky.

'It's been a strange day,' said Poke. 'Why don't we get some hot coffee and biscuits? We've got some things to tell you.'

They headed for the coffee house, walking close together. Poke and Leaf glanced nervously over their shoulders as they told Sky about the tent being trashed and invisible feet rustling leaves and visitors in the night trailing moonlight through the garden. The mist thickened, dimming the comforting lights of Home. It wasn't just the cold that made them shiver.

Chapter 5

Coat Tales

Early – but not too early – the next morning Poke was having breakfast at Whist's coffee house. Kite and Chip were there too, and Poke was telling them about Leaf's tent and the strange girl crying by the river.

'I have to find out what's going on,' said Poke, frowning as she poured more maple syrup on her pancakes.

Kite was still not convinced.

'I don't think anything is going on,' he said. 'No one's been hurt or anything. Maybe you were just having a bad dream. Maybe the wind blew everything around in Leaf's tent.'

Poke shook her head in frustration. 'I know there's something going on,' she said. 'You'll see.'

The three of them finished breakfast – Chip

finished two – and left the coffee house together. The morning mist had lifted and the sky was blue. The autumn air was crisp and fresh. The bitter chill of the previous afternoon had gone. It was hard to imagine any mysteries in Muddlemarsh.

They were approaching Slight's house. Slight was standing stock-still in the doorway. A lot of crashing noises were coming from inside the cottage.

Kite raised his eyebrows. 'Guess we'd better see if everything is OK,' he said, turning down the path towards Slight's door.

Slight was staring into the room. Poke, Kite and Chip peered around him. Something decidedly unusual was going on in there.

Slight's black magician's tailcoat was standing upright in the middle of the room, sleeves outstretched. As they watched, the coat bent left and then right and stumbled backwards for a few steps. The sleeves scrabbled at the fabric and an arc of cards flew out. Bending round and grabbing the hem, the coat seemed to be trying to turn itself inside out. Then the sleeves reached behind the back of the coat and waved about, feeling their way, before the coat wriggled and rushed backwards again, staggering unsteadily and bumping into the lamp. Coat and lamp crashed to the floor and lay still. A very tiny 'Ow' came from the pile of coat. Very cautiously, Slight edged into the room. He crouched down and carefully touched the coat. It felt warm and solid. He picked it up under the sleeves and held it at arm's length.

'What do you think's going on with your coat?' asked Kite from the doorway.

'Maybe my things have decided to work on some tricks without me,' said Slight, feeling a bit rejected by his props.

'What are you going to do with it?' Poke tilted her head towards the coat, which Slight was still holding gingerly.

'I think this needs at least, well, several Muddles,' Slight answered. 'And at this time of the morning most of them will be at the Common.'

'We'll come with you,' said Kite, and he and Poke walked alongside Slight. Poke was sure that the coat was still wriggling a bit. Chip strolled along a few steps behind.

Slight was right, most of the Muddles *had* gathered at the Common. Slight placed his bundle carefully on the ground. Instead of lying flat the coat huddled itself into a little crumpled heap. Then it sniffed. The Muddles gathered round, looking from Slight to the coat.

'Excellent magic trick, dude!' said Wave, grinning at Slight.

'It isn't a trick,' said Slight with dignity. 'Well, not unless my coat is doing tricks without me. I found my coat staggering around my cottage when I came home after breakfast.'

Wave nodded. 'Yep, know the feeling. Sometimes when I take my boardies off, they stand up all by themselves. Don't think it's magic though.'

Poke looked down at the shivering coat and then over at Kite, lifting her eyebrows and giving him a look which clearly said, 'So you still think nothing strange is happening in Muddlemarsh?' Kite whistled quietly and pretended not to notice.

The coat sniffed again and huddled itself more tightly together.

Poke, in detective mode, was walking around the coat, examining it from every side. 'I think,' she said finally, 'there is someone inside the coat.' Very carefully, Poke pulled the end of one of the sleeves, as if she was pulling it from the end of someone's arm. Suddenly the sleeve went limp. Poke did the same with the other sleeve. Then she took hold of the coat collar, lifted it up and pulled it aside.

Sitting huddled miserably on the grass, a shadowy, misty and barely visible green against it, was a girl. As she moved, her silky tunic and leggings changed colour in almost perfect camouflage. The girl lifted her head and looked anxiously around at the Muddles, her eyes wide and frightened.

'How do you do?' asked Slight politely. 'Let me introduce myself; Slight, Magician, at your service. And my coat too, of course.'

Wave stared at the girl, a deep frown taking hold of his face.

'Hey,' he said, 'didn't I see you catching some waves? But, sort of like "look, Ma, no board"? Really cool surfing!'

'Surfing?' said the girl, bewildered. 'What is surfing?'

Wave began to give a dry-land demonstration, making the motion of the waves, and then stretching out his arms and bending his knees in a pantomime of surfing. The rest of the Muddles gathered in closer, all talking at once. The girl stood up and looked in confusion from one to the other.

In the clear blue sky above, a single bird-shaped cloud passed over the sun. The Muddles shimmered. The girl blinked and looked around. All the same faces were there, but all the middle sections and the legs had somehow been mixed up and the surfer was wearing a scout uniform and the magician was wearing ballet tights and even the puppy was chasing its own duck tail. The girl moaned and sank back to the ground, pulling Slight's coat over her head.

Eventually she peeked out from under the coat. When nothing happened she stuck her head out. She couldn't help but stare at the strange-looking mixed Muddles.

'Where are you from?' asked Kite. 'You're not a

Beadle or a Myrmidot, and you're certainly not a Muddle.'

'A Muddle? No!' said the girl, trying not to stare at Kite's legs, which were actually, at that moment, Wave's. 'I'm a Moon Drinker.' She said this quite quietly, but her words silenced the Muddles.

They stepped back a pace or two and the exclamations flew among them. 'A Moon Drinker!' 'Imagine!' 'No!' 'I knew they were real!' 'But they're not real!' 'Are they real?'

'Of course we're real,' the girl answered, miffed. Then she smiled. 'Well, some of us didn't believe that the Muddle-Mix was real either,' she added. 'But I can see that it is.'

'I thought you were a Moon Drinker,' said Kite. 'I saw the Moon Drinkers one evening on the foothills of the High Mountains. And Moon Drinkers saved me from Wissen when he was going to experiment on me.'

'We hate Wissen,' said the girl, clenching her fists. 'He always makes trouble for us. We always try to stop him doing bad stuff if we can.'

'But why are you here?' enquired Poke, wanting to get to the bottom of the matter. 'Are there more Moon Drinkers with you?'

The girl shook her head. 'No, just me. I'm looking for our pearls. Someone has taken them.'

Once again all the Muddles started talking at once and asking questions.

'Shush,' said Kite. 'Let her talk.' He turned and smiled at the girl. 'What's your name?'

'Wenna,' she answered, smiling back at him.

There were polite introductions all round, and then Wenna told them more about the pearls going missing.

'We had them nearly four weeks ago at the full moon. I came back to the beach two nights ago, to make sure everything was prepared for the next full moon. I brought some more rose quartz with me, and I filled our silver ewer with water from the blue river. But I noticed our grinder was gone, and then I checked under the rock for our pearls and they were gone too. I found the grinder, but I've been looking for the pearls for the last two days. I've looked everywhere that I can think of and I can't find them, and I'll have to go back and tell everyone that our pearls are gone.'

'This must belong to you then,' said Sky, holding out her hand to Wenna and showing her the pearl she had found.

Wenna looked up in surprise. 'Where did this come from?' she asked.

Sky told her about seeing her on the bank of the Meddle and hearing her crying. 'And I was so sorry you ran away and I couldn't help you. But now we're friends?' Wenna nodded her head and smiled at Sky as she took the pearl.

'Why do you need the pearls?' asked Poke, who had been deep in thought.

Wenna went on to explain how they got their power from the moon.

'Why do you come to Muddlemarsh to collect pearls? Can't you get them where you live?'

'Yes, but the best pearls are here, and anyway we need to use the water from the blue river,' Wenna explained. 'We usually get it where it flows near the beach, because we've always been afraid to come into your town.'

'The River Meddle.' Poke nodded, though she was still not sure she had got to the bottom of things. 'What happens if you don't have enough pearls?' she asked.

'If we don't drink the pearl mix under the full moon we'll just keep fading away until we go into a deep sleep. Maybe forever. We might even die!' said Wenna tragically. 'That's why I was in Slight's coat. I was looking for the pearls that had gone missing and then, I don't know how it happened, but I sort of got stuck backwards inside the lining and the coat wouldn't let me go.'

Slight nodded sagely. 'A magician's coat is a very tricky thing, if you don't know how to handle it,' he said.

Wenna looked a bit embarrassed. 'And there's one other thing. I was looking for the pearls in someone's tent, and I guess I made a bit of a mess. But I did clean up the coffee beans,' she added, hoping this might be something in her favour.

'What coffee beans?' asked Poke.

'When I was looking for the pearls I accidentally knocked over a sack of coffee beans. But I did sweep them all up and put them back in the sack.'

('Well, that explains the bad coffee at Whist's,' thought Poke.)

Poke was looking at the way Wenna subtly changed colour to match her surroundings.

'Did you follow me the other night?' she asked suddenly. 'I thought I heard someone kicking the leaves behind me. But when I looked round I couldn't see anyone.'

Wenna nodded. 'Yes, but I was too afraid to speak to you so I hid against the tree.'
('I knew it,' Calamity growled, wagging her duck tail. 'I knew there was someone under that tree.')

'And were you in my house last night?' asked Poke.

Wenna nodded. 'I didn't know what else to do,' she said, looking up at Poke. 'I have to find our pearls and I don't know where they've gone.'

'Well, we don't have your pearls,' said Kite, 'and we don't know who could've taken them.'

Everyone was silent, considering the mysterious disappearance of the pearls. Having considered it very carefully, they were none the wiser.

'We need to get to the bottom of this mystery,' said Poke. 'It could take some serious detective work.' She looked again at Kite. 'I knew there was something strange going on. I just had -'

'We know, a gut feeling,' said Kite, finishing her sentence. Poke ignored him.

'What are you going to do now?' asked Sky, looking at Wenna.

Wenna shook her head. 'I don't know. If the pearls aren't here, I'll have to go back to the island and tell the rest of the Moon Drinkers. Now we only have today to collect enough pearls for the full moon tomorrow night. But I don't know if we can do it, and then maybe we will all just fade away and die!'

Wave shook his head slowly and looked grim. 'Man,' he said, 'you dudes are in big trouble.'

The Muddles looked at one another. It was Leaf who finally spoke. 'I think we need to call a Town Meeting. The Moon Drinkers need help.'

The Muddles nodded and murmured their agreement. They would call a Town Meeting.

Grunge rang the brass bell that hung in the centre of the Quad. Soon almost every Muddle in Home had gathered on the Common.

Leaf was the Muddles' Town Leader for the week. She stood on a rock so she could be seen and heard by everyone. The Muddles who had not been there when Slight brought Wenna to the Common were very excited (and a bit nervous) at having a Moon Drinker in their midst. Most of the Muddles had believed that Moon Drinkers were just a strange and scary part of the old tales.

'We have gathered here for a very important reason,' said Leaf, going on to explain about the Moon Drinkers and their pearls.

'So now we have to decide whether or not we can help the Moon Drinkers,' she announced. 'Who will stand and say?'

'I will stand and say,' answered Kite, standing up next to Leaf. 'And we will let the sticks decide.'

Each Muddle took one yellow and one blue stick from their pockets.

'I stand here and say,' said Kite solemnly, 'shall we help the Moon Drinkers?'

Sticks flew into the air and clattered to the ground. Wave's stick clattered on his head first. 'Must be something wrong with my stick,' he said to himself as he picked it up and studied it carefully.

Leaf looked at the ground in front of her. All the sticks were yellow.

'The sticks have decided; we will help the Moon Drinkers,' Leaf told the assembled Muddles.

'Cool,' said Wave. 'Um, how?'

Sky looked at Wenna. 'How can we help?'

'Well,' said Wenna slowly, 'I haven't found the missing pearls, so the Moon Drinkers will have to come back to the beach today and collect more.

This is our last chance before the full moon tomorrow night. We have to rest on the day of the full moon.'

'Well then,' said Sky, 'that's settled. We will help you collect pearls.'

Wenna looked a bit doubtful. 'Have you ever gone diving for pearls before?'

Sky shook her head. 'No,' she said cheerfully, 'but I'm sure we can help.'

All around Wenna the Muddles were smiling and nodding reassuringly. "Of course", "Definitely", "Happy to help", they were saying. Wenna smiled back, feeling much more hopeful.

She got up to leave. 'I will go back to our island and tell them what has happened and we will all come back to the beach later today and collect more pearls.'

'Wanna a ride to the beach?' Wave asked her. 'I'll take you on my bike.'

'Yes please,' said Wenna.

Wave got on his bike. Wenna tried not to notice that instead of his usual sandals, Wave was pedalling with red pointy-toed shoes. Wenna jumped lightly onto the handle bar and stood balancing there.

'You going to sit down?' Wave asked.

Wenna shook her head and laughed. 'No, thank you.'

Wave was still looking a bit worried. 'You sure you aren't going to fall off?'

'Of course I won't. Let's go,' said Wenna.

Wave shrugged. 'OK.' The little bells on the tips of Japes's pointy shoes tinkled prettily as he pedalled.

The other Muddles drifted away from the Common. Poke sat talking with Chip and Kite. Chip, as usual, was not saying much.

'Who would want to steal the Moon Drinkers' pearls?' said Poke. 'Maybe someone wants the Moon Drinkers to die!'

'Or maybe just someone who likes pearls,' said Kite.

Poke narrowed her eyes and stared over the Quad, deep in thought.

'Sooner or later we'll find out,' she said. 'There's something bad going on.'

Kite threw a lump of grass at her.

'You know I'm right,' she yelled at Kite.

'Yeah, well, maybe you'll get a prize,' Kite yelled back.

Chip just looked at them and grinned.

Chapter 6

Potions and Plots

In a wild part of the forest, in a hut made of tree trunks and stone, Wissen was deep in thought. A neglected fire smouldered in the hearth. The smell of smoke, laced with potions brewing and a hint of old socks, filled the room. A bright yellow canary flew in and nearly passed out from the smell. It fluttered about, crashed into walls and then fell dizzily off a rafter into Wissen's lap. He picked it up and tossed it out the window. It flew away, still slightly unsteady.

Wissen was experimenting with the pearls he had stolen from the Moon Drinkers. The pearls were almost as exciting as the black powder. Wissen looked around his hut. Iridescent bubbles rose from the oily liquid boiling in a black enamel bucket. In a large-bottomed flask a clear liquid sparkled enticingly. Gas was filling a silk bag tied tightly over the neck of a brown two-handled bottle. Wissen was very pleased with himself.

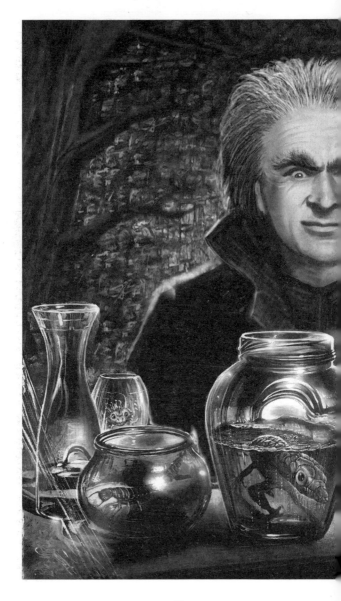

Pleased, but not satisfied. Wissen had more experiments planned and the pearls were almost gone. He guessed that the Moon Drinkers would have to replenish their store of pearls before the full moon. Wissen wanted those pearls. He would go back to the beach and steal them, he decided. He planned and plotted, wondering how he could take the pearls from a large group of Moon Drinkers who would, presumably, guard them much more carefully now.

But, he told himself, he didn't have much time. Tomorrow night the moon would be full.

Wissen had not forgotten the purple haze that had overpowered the cat. He bit his thumbnail and wondered … It was risky but it just might work.

Reluctantly – remembering the headache – Wissen mixed the last of the pearls with the black powder and ground them together. He should've taken the Moon Drinkers' grinder; his was much slower. Wissen filled his flask with water from the spring and added the pearly black powder. The next night, when the moon was full, he would fly down to the beach and take the precious pearls.

Wissen completed the rest of his preparations.

Thinking they might come in handy, he packed up several of his experimental pearl mixtures and dropped them in behind the driver's seat of his flying machine. He didn't even notice the cat, still lying motionless in the back.

Chapter 7

Deep Pearls

While Wissen was plotting to steal the pearls from the Moon Drinkers, the Muddles were sitting on the beach. They were waiting for Wenna and the Moon Drinkers. Weed the duck had heard that swimming might be required and had offered his services. He hadn't been expecting to swim in the ocean and was nervously watching the high waves rushing into the beach. To a small duck, they looked very high indeed.

The afternoon was a little chilly, and the Muddles sat close to their campfire. When they weren't talking, they stared into the heart of the fire, or out over the ocean. The waves rolled steadily into the shore, breaking in sprays of foam before throwing themselves onto the sand.

Close to the fire, Grunge, the Muddles finest – and only – musician was plucking at the strings of his guitar. Crimson was sitting next to him, examining her red fire officer's jacket. She was relieved to see it had dried out beautifully after its ocean dip with Wave.

Poke was sitting away from Kite. She hadn't forgiven him for not believing her about the strange goings-on in Muddlemarsh. Kite looked at Poke. He got up and walked around the fire to sit beside her.

'You know what?' he said, sitting down next to her. 'You may not have noticed, but some weird stuff has been happening in Muddlemarsh. I thought all along that something wasn't quite right.'

Poke started to yell at him and then saw him grinning. She laughed and gently pushed him over on the sand.

'Don't tell me,' she said. 'You just had a gut feeling.'

'Yep,' he answered, rolling over on the sand.

The rest of the Muddles were discussing pearl fishing.

'Maybe weese have to squeeze the oysters and the

pearls pop out, like,' said Patch.

'Maybe the oysters spit them out if they're frightened,' suggested Chip.

'How do you frighten an oyster?' asked Lift, one of the very young Muddles.

'Tell them ghost stories,' Grunge answered, grinning.

'But they don't have any ears,' said Lift, and the rest of the Muddles laughed. Grunge looked down at Lift.

'A very good point. We will have to try something else,' he said solemnly.

Poke had been watching for the Moon Drinkers.

'I think they're coming,' she said, shading her eyes. She could see waves topped with uneven peaks coming towards the beach. The waves came closer and the peaks became Moon Drinkers, riding the waves. Their hair flowed with the bright spray in a silvery golden stream in the sunlight.

The Moon Drinkers glided onto the beach. They waved at the Muddles and walked towards their fire.

Poke looked carefully at them. They all wore the same long silky tunics over leggings as she had seen on Wenna. They didn't look wet. As they stood near the fire, the silky fabric flowed and flickered in a constantly changing blend of smoky reds and oranges.

Wenna introduced a very tall Moon Drinker to the rest of the Muddles. 'This is Melwyn,' she said. The rest of the Muddles and the Moon Drinkers introduced themselves.

Poke watched Sky and Melwyn talking, their heads close together. She suddenly thought how alike they were; tall, straight and beautiful, with hair curling around their necks and their faces luminous. Melwyn reached out and touched the black pearls in Sky's ears. As the two of them talked and smiled, Poke was sure they were sharing some magical secret.

Then everyone sat down around the fire and coffee and sandwiches were handed around.

At their first sip of coffee the Moon Drinkers shuddered. They looked at each other. What was this horrible drink? Watching their faces, Whist suddenly laughed. 'Well,' she said, 'I guess maybe you have to be born a Muddle to enjoy coffee. But there is plenty of food to go round.' The Moon Drinkers smiled gratefully at her.

'Well, me buckos,' said Patch, his pirate hat nodding up and down as he looked around the group, 'ain't no good wasting time gabbin', like, cos weese has pearls to catch. Now,' he said, turning to look at Melwyn, 'whatcha be thinkin' that weese should all be doin' to get them pearls?'

Melwyn explained that the Moon Drinkers swam out to sea and dived to the floor of the ocean to harvest the pearl oysters.

'We bring the oysters to the beach and open them to collect their pearls. Then we throw the oysters back into the water.'

She looked doubtfully at the Muddles. 'Can you swim?' she asked.

Some of the Muddles shook their heads. Crimson and Sky nodded; they were both strong swimmers.

'Happy to paddle on my board,' said Wave.

Everyone looked down expectantly at Weed. 'I guess I can swim too,' he quacked.

'And we can all help with collecting the pearls from the shells,' Kite added.

'Well, you'll need this then,' said Melwyn, handing him something that looked like a cross between a knife and a screwdriver. 'Use it to open the oyster shells, but be careful not to hurt yourself.'

Muddles and Moon Drinkers walked down to the water's edge. Sky waded waist-deep and dived gracefully into the deep green heart of a wave.

Crimson hesitated, looking down at her bright red jacket. 'At least I know it has survived seawater before,' she consoled herself.

Weed waddled to the edge of the waves. He glanced up at Crimson. 'I'm not sure if I'm an ocean-going duck,' he said doubtfully. The waves looked very big.

'Of course you are,' she said reassuringly. 'You're the best swimmer we have.'

'If you say so ... Well, here goes.' He closed his eyes and jumped onto a retreating wave.

The Moon Drinkers followed, riding the waves out to deep water.

'Man, that's cool,' said Wave to Poke, who was standing next to him. 'Wish I could do that.' He lay on his board and started to paddle out after them.

'Wait,' Whist called out. 'You'll need something to put the oysters in.' She handed Wave her picnic basket. Wave balanced it on the front of his board and paddled out over the waves.

From the shore, Poke could see Wave, a long way out, lying on his board and holding the picnic basket. The first of the pearl divers to surface was Sky. Smiling, she dropped a handful of oyster shells into the picnic basket and dived back under the water. Every now and again, a Moon Drinker would rise up from the water with their catch and Wave would put the oysters into the basket. But it was easy to see that Sky was collecting by far the most oysters.

Crimson and Weed were working together. Weed would dive deep down to the floor of the ocean and bring back an oyster to Crimson, who would then swim over and give it to Wave.

After an hour or so Wave paddled into shore, carefully balancing the basket on his surfboard. Wenna rode the wave beside him. When they got to the shore, Wave put his board under one arm, carrying the heavy basket with the other. He tipped the oysters onto the sand near the Muddles.

Kite picked up his first oyster and tried to prise it open with the tool that Melwyn had given him. It was a lot harder than he had expected.

Wenna sat down next to him. 'Not like that. Like this,' she said, finding a small gap in the shell and inserting the tool. She gave it an expert twist and the shell popped open, revealing a tiny pearl.

After a few more tries, Kite was starting to get the hang of it.

'I'd better go and collect more oysters,' said Wenna, standing up.

Patch looked over at Wave. 'You'd better be goin' with her, young 'un. Shore leave's over,' he said,

giving Wave a nudge.

Wave tucked the board under his arm and headed back into the ocean, taking the basket with him.

Kite and the rest of the Muddles sat on the sand, Kite opening the oyster shells and the others searching them for pearls. Not every oyster yielded a pearl, but they were starting to get a nice little pile of them. They placed them carefully in Slight's tall magician's hat for safe keeping.

Wave was carrying the last basket of oysters onto the beach. Sky, Crimson, Weed and the Moon Drinkers were following close behind.

The sky was dotted with loose clouds, but one of them was racing faster than the others across the sun. The Muddles shimmered and mixed. Wave continued up the beach without breaking his stride, even though he was now striding with Grunge's legs. Unfortunately he was no longer carrying the basket of oysters. His middle section was a crisp white nurse's uniform – Bright's of course – and carrying a roll of bandages.

Only a few Moon Drinkers had ever seen a Mix happening. To most of them it was still a not-quite-believable legend. They stopped in surprise at the edge of the water as the Mix passed over. It was a few seconds before they noticed that Wave no longer had the basket. They hurried up to the group of Muddles. Wave was looking down dejectedly at his hands.

'Oh man, that was the biggest catch of the day,' he said, shaking his head.

'But where did it go?' asked Melwyn, confused.

Wave shrugged his shoulders and Bright's red cape bunched up around his neck.

'Could be anywhere,' he said. 'Never know who's gonna get what in a Mix.'

The Moon Drinkers looked at each other in dismay. They needed every last pearl.

Grunge came loping down the sand dunes towards them. He was holding the basket of oyster shells.

'Looking for this?' he asked, holding out the basket. 'I got Wave's middle,' he explained to the somewhat bemused Moon Drinkers.

'Yes,' said Melwyn, quickly taking it from him and clutching it tightly with both hands.

Sitting down, they opened the last of the oysters, adding each precious pearl to the pile in Slight's hat. When they were done, Slight picked up his hat, shaking the sand off before handing it to Melwyn.

Melwyn smiled at him as she took the hat from his (well, Whist's) hands. She looked down into the hat and her legs nearly collapsed under her. The hat was empty.

'Where are the pearls?' she asked in a panic.

Slight peered into the hat.

'Goodness me,' he said. 'Where can they have gone?'

Slight ran his hand around the brim of his top hat. A bright rope of scarves trailed behind his hand, curling in a spiral of coloured gossamer inside the brim. Slight tugged on the scarves and they broke free of the hat and floated onto the sand. The pearls were once again lying safe in the bottom of the hat.

'Magician's hat, you know,' he explained.

'Of course,' said Melwyn, wondering what other surprises were in store and feeling slightly nervous.

'Perhaps the pearls would be safer here,' she said, taking the hat and tipping the pearls into the soft leather pouch she carried. She hung the pouch around her neck. 'We will keep the pearls safe with us until the full moon tomorrow night, when we return for the Moon Ceremony.'

'Will you have enough pearls?' asked Sky.

'I hope so,' said Melwyn, looking a bit worried, but then smiling. 'Thank you all so much for helping us. You know, Sky, you seemed to have a knack for finding the best pearl oysters.'

'I could feel them calling to me,' Sky answered dreamily.

Melwyn looked up to the hollow where the silver ewer, filled with water from the Meddle, still stood on top of the flat rock. The grinder was next to it.

'I think the grinder and the ewer will be safe until tomorrow night. Whoever took the pearls last time didn't think they were worth stealing.'

The Moon Drinkers and the Muddles said their goodbyes. The Moon Drinkers skipped into the waves and headed out to sea. Sky watched them until they disappeared from sight.

Chapter 8

Purple Mist

It was the night of the full moon. Under silver moonbeams the Moon Drinkers rode the waves onto the beach at Muddlemarsh. Melwyn led the group to their hollow in the sand. The silver ewer and the grinder were still there, undisturbed.

They sat cross-legged in their usual circle. Melwyn was nervous; she knew that they had barely enough pearls to go around. She looked at the Moon Drinkers, staring up at her trustingly. She started to speak, her voice clear and sweet.

'You know that when someone stole our pearls our lives were threatened. Thanks to our new friends, the Muddles, we have managed to collect the pearls for tonight's Moon Ceremony. I don't know if we will have enough pearls to draw the moonlight to us. But we will share the pearls equally and share the same fate, whether it is good or bad.'

The Moon Drinkers nodded solemnly. Melwyn carefully lifted the two pouches – one of pearls and one of rose quartz – over her head. She stretched out her hand to pass them to her two companions by the grinder. A shadow passed over the Moon Drinkers. Looking up anxiously, they saw a large dark oval pass overhead. It circled downwards and landed on the beach not far from the hollow. Fear gripped the Moon Drinkers as they looked to where the object had landed. Then their worst fears were realised. Wissen, tall, dark and menacing, appeared over the lip of the hollow. He stood on the rim, blocking the moon, and his shadow spread itself over the Moon Drinkers below.

'Well, well,' he sneered, looking down at the pouch in Melwyn's hand. 'I see that once again you have quite a catch of pearls for me.' He held out his hand. 'Give them to me,' he commanded, stepping down into the hollow. In the moonlight they could see his breath trailing purple from his mouth.

Melwyn stepped back. 'No!' she said defiantly. The Moon Drinkers gathered protectively around her.

'Yes!' Wissen stepped closer to them, his nostrils

flaring as he took a deep, deep breath. He opened his mouth and exhaled, forcing out his poison breath. Purple vapour wrapped itself around the heads of the Moon Drinkers. Those closest to him swayed and fell lifeless to the ground. Wissen moved to Melwyn and reached out to grab her by the throat. But Melwyn, quick as a moonbeam, caught his arm in mid-air and wrenched it down. Wissen cried out in pain. He leaned his face into hers and his breath came out in an angry purple stream. The violet mist snaked towards her. It twisted around her neck and crawled into her mouth and nose. She couldn't breathe. Despair filled her as she sank to her knees and toppled to the ground.

The Moon Drinkers closest to Melwyn had taken the full force of Wissen's breath. They were lying on the ground, still and cold. Those who had been further away were sick and dazed. They crouched on their hands and knees, disorientated and unseeing. Wissen reached for the pouch of pearls and put it in his pocket; there was no one to stop him now. He turned and climbed out of the hollow then headed over the top of the dunes.

Wissen gave a self-satisfied smirk. He had won. He blew a few smoke rings. The smoky purple 'Os' drifted around like letters looking for the alphabet. Wissen hiccupped. Little purple puffs popped out of his mouth. Soon they paled to lavender. The purple breath was fading as he came over the top of the last sand dune near his machine.

And came face to face with the Muddles.

Kite was the first to speak. 'You!' he said, recognising Wissen.

'Yes, you're right there,' agreed Wissen. 'Don't tell me you're not happy to see me?'

'What do you want?' Kite asked, afraid but still standing his ground.

'Mmm, let me see, I think I came to collect some pearls to continue my experiments,' said Wissen, holding up the pouch. 'And while we're here, there is the tiny but really annoying matter of you' – Wissen emphasised his point by stabbing his finger at Kite – 'stealing and wrecking my flying machine.'

'Well, I didn't mean to wreck it, exactly,' said Kite. 'Anyway, it was your fault really for kidnapping me and trying to do experiments on me and my friends.'

'My scientific experiments are more important than you,' said Wissen dismissively.

'What's wrong with your breath?' asked Poke. 'It's a bit purple.'

Wissen exhaled, squeezing out the last purple wisps. 'So it is,' he said, moving in closer to the Muddles. 'Well, it's been marvellous to chat, but I really must be going.' He bent over Kite and Poke and breathed heavily over them. A few lavender wisps drifted into their faces. They swayed dizzily for a moment. And as they did, Wissen darted past the dazed Muddles. He leapt over the side of his machine and started the motor. It purred softly and the machine lifted off the sand. Wissen and the pearls were out of reach.

Chapter 9

Sparkling Moonlight

The Muddles huddled around Poke and Kite, who were still pale and dizzy. Sky put her arms around them. Almost immediately the dizziness left them and their heads cleared.

'We need to find the Moon Drinkers and see if they're OK,' said Sky, looking worried. The Muddles walked over the sand to the Moon Drinkers' hollow and looked down. Most of the Moon Drinkers were lying motionless on the sand, their moonlit glow almost gone. The rest were swaying unsteadily or crouched down on the ground.

'No!' shouted Sky, racing down the slope towards them. The sight of Melwyn, lying pale and still, brought her to a stop. Tears streamed down Sky's face as she knelt beside her. She lifted Melwyn's head on to her lap and stroked her pale face, then she leaned down and kissed Melwyn's pale forehead.

A tiny plume of purple drifted out of Melwyn's mouth.

'Look,' said Poke. 'I think she's breathing.'

Sky bent her ear to Melwyn's mouth, trying to feel her breath. Melwyn coughed as a great purple fume gushed out of her mouth. The cloud swirled towards Sky's head, then curled around her ears and disappeared.

Sky put her hands to her ears. 'My ears are hot,' she said in surprise.

Poke had been watching closely. 'Your earrings are glowing,' she said, leaning in closely to look at them. Then she shook her head in disbelief. 'It's your earrings! Your earrings are absorbing the purple stuff. It looks like they're just sucking it right in.'

Melwyn coughed again and sat up. Sky gave her a hug and then went to help the other Moon Drinkers. Her black pearl earrings drew forth Wissen's purple poison from each of them until her earrings were glowing and her ears were burning hot.

When the last Moon Drinker had been revived, Sky came back to Melwyn. Melwyn was looking sadly at her group.

'I don't know what will happen to us,' she said quietly. 'Our pearls are gone.'

Wave's face appeared over the top of the sand dunes that ringed the hollow.

'Maybe not,' he said, grinning. 'You gotta see this.'

Muddles and Moon Drinkers scrambled and skipped out of the hollow and followed Wave.

'Look up, dudes,' he said, pointing to the dark sky.

Circling round and round over their heads, the polished metal catching the moonlight, was Wissen's flying machine. They could hear Wissen cursing.

'Why is he doing that?' asked Melwyn. 'Why doesn't he just go?'

Wave pointed at a large rock. A rope was tied

around it. Following the line of the rope skywards, they could see Wissen's machine tethered underneath to the other end of the rope.

'Patch and Chip did it,' said Wave proudly. 'They sneaked over to his machine when he was mouthin' off and blowin' on Kite and Poke. Chip had his rope on his lumberjack belt. Course, Patch tied the knots.'

More cursing could be heard from Wissen. A large object flew over the side of the flying machine and thudded on the soft sand. It was the two-handled brown bottle. The flat-bottomed flask came next. The liquid inside sparkled as it caught the moonlight. The cork held fast and it landed on the sand without losing a drop.

'What's he doing?' asked Melwyn.

'Well now, I expects he's a-tryin' to lighten the load and break free from that rope, like,' said Patch, looking up at Wissen's machine. 'But weese tied them knots real good.'

Grunge was calling up to Wissen. 'Hey, Wissen, you may as well give up now. We're not going to

untie the rope 'til you throw the pearls down.'

'Yeah,' said Kite, 'you don't wanna keep going round and round 'til you run out of fuel and crash. Your machine already looks a bit dented.'

This time Wissen's head appeared over the side of the machine. He was shaking his fist and cursing. A large dark bundle flew out of the machine. It landed on the soft sand near Poke's feet.

'It's a cat!' said Poke, shocked. 'I think it's dead.' She picked it up and held it to her chest.

Still the machine went round and round. They could hear the motor straining as Wissen tried to break free of the rope. It was no good; he knew he was beaten. Cursing again, he threw the pouch of pearls over the side of the machine.

'Thank-ee,' said Patch, strolling over to untie the rope. Wissen was still using full throttle and with the sudden release from the rope the machine shot up almost vertically into the air and did a backwards loop. A few more things fell out onto the sand. Wissen was very nearly one of them. The machine righted itself and headed unsteadily over the cliff tops, the rope trailing behind.

Kite ran over to pick up the pouch of pearls and handed them to Melwyn. She was laughing and crying and shaking.

'Thank you,' she said. 'All of you.' The rest of the Moon Drinkers joined her in thanking the Muddles.

The Muddles insisted that they were glad to have helped.

'Weese had a bit of fun-like with that Wissen and the rope as well,' grinned Patch.

Poke was still holding the cat and stroking its motionless body. 'Poor cat!' she thought. 'How could Wissen be so mean?'

Sky had an idea. She rubbed her face against the soft fur. The cat stirred, and gave a purple hiccup. Then it stretched and began to purr, nestling into Poke's arms.

'I guess Wissen purpled the cat too,' said Poke.

'Well now,' said Melwyn. 'It's time for us to continue the Moon ceremony.' She turned to face the Muddles. 'Won't you please come with us?'

They all walked back to the sandy hollow and the Moon Drinkers continued their interrupted preparations.

Melwyn was looking into the pouch that Wissen had thrown out of the machine. She frowned as she counted the pearls out into her hand.

'There are six pearls missing,' she said. 'We're doomed.'

'Wait,' said Kite, and ran back to the sand where Wissen had thrown his bottles and jars overboard. He gathered as many as he could hold and ran back to the hollow.

'Here,' he said, panting as he handed them to the Moon Drinkers. 'Wissen said he was experimenting with the pearls. Maybe there are still some in these bottles?'

Gingerly they opened the bottles. Mostly they smelt really bad. Only the clear liquid that sparkled in the flask smelt sweet. A few ground-up pearls were sprinkled at the bottom of the flask. When Kite held it up, gold and silver specks, suspended in the liquid, glittered in the moonlight.

'Maybe you could use this?' Sky suggested hesitantly.

'I don't know,' said Melwyn doubtfully. 'I don't trust anything that comes from Wissen.'

'What choice do we have?' argued Wenna. She lowered her voice. 'You know what could happen if we don't have enough pearls.'

Wave leaned over and stuck his finger in the flask and licked off the sticky liquid.

'Tastes pretty good,' he said, licking his lips. He waited a minute or two. 'I feel pretty good too.'

So the Moon Drinkers ground their pearls and rose quartz, mixed them with water from the River Meddle, and added a generous splash of Wissen's sparkling pearl cocktail.

They all waited anxiously. The moonbeams brightened in a circle around the Moon Drinkers and then faded. The Moon Drinkers glowed more than ever and their eyes were bright.

'Do you feel OK?' Kite asked.

Wenna nodded and smiled. 'We feel wonderful,' she answered.

The faces of all the Muddles broke into wide grins, and each and every Muddle burst out laughing.

'Perhaps you should have a really good look at yourselves,' said Sky, still laughing.

The Moon Drinkers turned and looked at each other, glowing with inner moonlight. But there was something different this time. Each of them glittered, dusted with silver and gold.

'Very nice,' said Poke. 'It must have been those gold and silver specks in that liquid.'

'Oh man,' said Wave, slapping the side of his forehead, 'I didn't know we were dressing up.'

Then the Moon Drinkers laughed too.

The Muddles and the Moon Drinkers sat on the beach under the moon and talked and sang and laughed. Chip chopped some kindling with his tomahawk and Leaf made a campfire. Sky and Melwyn sat close together in the moonlight, talking quietly. Poke watched the two of them for a moment. Under the moonlight, Sky was more beautiful than ever. Poke hugged the cat more tightly and the cat purred and rubbed itself against Poke.

Kite came and sat down next to her and rather absent-mindedly stroked the cat. He grinned at Poke and she dug her elbow into his ribs. She was glad he was there.

Whist produced coffee and biscuits. The Moon Drinkers, while politely declining the coffee, showed themselves to be very partial to the honey-nuts. All in all, it was a great party and everyone had a good time. But every great party has to end. The moon set and the sky grew lighter. It was time for the Moon Drinkers to go back to their island.

Muddles and Moon Drinkers said their goodbyes, and the Muddles stood on the sand and waved, watching the Moon Drinkers disappear over the sea. They all agreed that it had been a scary and wonderful night.

Everyone except Wissen, who woke with a nasty headache. He groaned and pulled the blankets over his head. Cursing Muddles and Moon Drinkers and pearls, he swore he would have his revenge. He was not finished with them yet.

THE END